OLIVIA™
Becomes a Vet

adapted by Alex Harvey
based on the screenplay written by Patricia Resnick
illustrated by Jared Osterhold

Ready-to-Read

Simon Spotlight
New York   London   Toronto   Sydney

Based on the TV series *OLIVIA*™ as seen on Nickelodeon™

SIMON SPOTLIGHT
An imprint of Simon & Schuster Children's Publishing Division
1230 Avenue of the Americas, New York, New York 10020
Copyright © 2011 Silver Lining Productions Limited (a Chorion company). All rights reserved.
OLIVIA™ and © 2011 Ian Falconer. All rights reserved, including the right of
reproduction in whole or in part in any form. SIMON SPOTLIGHT, READY-TO-READ,
and colophon are registered trademarks of Simon & Schuster, Inc.
For information about special discounts for bulk purchases, please contact
Simon & Schuster Special Sales at 1-866-506-1949 or business@simonandschuster.com.
Manufactured in the United States of America 1011 LAK
2 3 4 5 6 7 8 9 10
ISBN 978-1-4424-2860-7(hc)
ISBN 978-1-4424-2859-1(pbk)

"Bernie might be sick,"
Julian tells Olivia. "He will
not eat. I keep giving him
flies, but he just sits there."

"I know what to do,"
says Olivia.

They take Bernie
to the vet for a checkup.
"What do you feed him?"
asks the vet.
"Flies," Julian says.

The vet nods her head.
"I think I know what
is wrong," she says.
"I will be right back."

"Do not worry, Bernie,"
Julian tells his lizard.
"She is a very good doctor."

When the vet returns,
she feeds him a cricket.
And Bernie eats it!

"I think Bernie was bored just eating flies," the vet explains.

When Olivia gets home
she tells her mom
she wants to be a vet.
"That is wonderful,"
Mom says.

Olivia decides to start
right away.
She gets her vet bag
and instruments.

"How do you feel, Perry?"
she asks her dog.
"Hmm . . . cold nose,"
says Olivia.
"That is a good sign."

But before Olivia can do
anything else, Perry runs
away!

"Perry, you are not done
with your checkup!"

Then Olivia decides that Edwin has a pretend illness. "You have furry-foot-itis," she says. "You need an ice pack."

Olivia begins to dream about her life as a vet. "Here is the problem," she tells a lion. "It was your sweet tooth!"

"Come on and blow!"
she says to an elephant.
"You will feel better."
"I have something to
fix you up," she tells
a camel. "Honey!"

The camel is very thankful.

"I feel better!" it says.

"Olivia is the best vet
ever!"

When Olivia finds Perry,
he has red sticky jam on
him.

"You must have strawberry
jam disease," Olivia says.

Olivia and Ian wash
Perry, and the jam
comes right off.
"You are cured, Perry!"
Olivia says.

Just then Olivia's mom says
that Edwin had an accident.
"Was it a little puddle under
the table?" asks Olivia.

"Yes," Mom says.

"Oh, it was just water from the ice pack," Olivia says.

At night Olivia's mom
tucks her in.
Mom starts to say,
"You are a special—"

"Vet?" says Olivia.

"Girl," Mom says.

"Good night, Olivia."